CLASSIC COLLECTION

BLACK BEAUTY

ANNA SEWELL

Adapted by anne rooney · Illustrated by matt baker

SWEET WATER PRESS

My First Home

My earliest memories are happy ones. I lived on my mother's milk and played with six other colts in a meadow with a pool filled with water lilies and a stream. As soon as I was old enough to eat grass, my mother went to work and I passed my days galloping and playing with my companions. Sometimes our play was rough.

"The colts that live here are the colts of carthorses," my mother said one day. "They have not learned their manners. I hope you will grow up gentle and good, do your work with a good will, and never bite or kick."

Our master was a kind man. He fed us well and kept us warm and safe. He stopped the local boys throwing sticks at us. I knew nothing but kindness toward horses until I was two years old. Then I saw something I will never forget.

It was a cold spring morning and we were all in the field when the sound of dogs barking was carried to us on the wind.

"They have found a hare," my mother said. "We will see the hunt."

Sure enough, we soon saw the dogs. They burst from the woods, leaped over a stream, and were rapidly followed by men on horseback.

The hare was cornered and killed by the hounds. We were so busy watching this scene that we did not notice the fuss by the stream.

2

Two horses and riders had fallen jumping over the stream. One of the riders lay unmoving and his horse was groaning on the grass. Men rushed around, fetching a doctor and taking news to the young lad's father, Squire Gordon. Then my master carried the limp rider away. Another man checked the horse and found that his leg was broken. They shot the poor horse in the head.

A few days later, we heard the church bell toll and watched mourners going to the boy's funeral. He had broken his neck in the fall and died.

Despite the tragedy, life for us went on as usual. By the time I was four, I was a fine, handsome young horse with a smooth black coat. I had a pretty white star on my forehead and one white foot.

When I was four years old, it was time for me to leave my home. Before he sold me, my master needed to break me in—to get me ready for work. I had to get used to wearing a saddle and a bit. The saddle was not too bad, but the bit was terrible. You can't imagine how it feels to have a hard bar of metal forced into your mouth!

Next, I had horseshoes fitted so that I could walk over the hard roads. They didn't hurt, but made my legs feel heavy. There was a crupper, too, which was a harness that held my tail high. It was uncomfortable, but there was nothing to be done about it—that was the life of a horse.

Squire Gordon

In the last weeks before I was sold, I learned to pull a carriage and was sent to a field near a railroad line, so that I could get used to the roar of the trains. I shall never forget the first train that went by—I was terrified of the screaming black monster that hurtled along the end of the field. I galloped to the far side of the meadow and stood snorting with astonishment and fear. I soon learned, though, that it never strayed from its path and could do me no harm.

Often, I went in harness with my mother. She took the chance to give me advice, saying the better I behaved, the better I would be treated.

"There are many kinds of men," she warned. "There are good thoughtful men, like our master, but there are also bad, cruel men, who should never be allowed to own a horse. Then there are foolish men, ignorant and careless, who ruin horses. They don't mean to do it, but they do it all the same. I hope you will fall into good hands; but a horse never knows who may buy him."

In early May, a man came to collect me to take me to Squire Gordon's stables at Birtwick Hall.

My master said, "Good-bye, Darkie; be a good horse, and always do your best."

I could not say good-bye, but I put my nose into his hand. He patted me kindly and I left my first home.

6

Squire Gordon's park was large, with a paddock, an old orchard, and several stables. My stable was roomy, with four stalls and a window. It had a low rack for hay and a manger for corn. It was called a loosebox, because the horse in it was not tied up, but left loose.

In the stall next to mine stood a fat gray pony with a thick mane and tail and a pretty head. He said his name was Merrylegs, and that he took the young ladies for rides and pulled the carriage of the lady of the house. Just then, a bad-tempered chestnut mare, called Ginger, peered over from another stall.

"So it is you who have turned me out of my box," she grumbled. "It is a very strange thing for a colt like you to come and cast a lady out of her own home."

I told her that it had not been my choice, and that I only wanted to live in peace. In the afternoon, though, when Ginger was taken out, Merrylegs told me more about her.

"Ginger has a bad habit of biting and snapping," Merrylegs said. "One day she bit James, the stableboy, on the arm and made him bleed, so Miss Flora and Miss Jessie are afraid to come into the stable. I hope they will now come again, if you do not bite or snap. It is just a bad habit; she says no one was ever kind to her. But John, the groom, does all he can to please her, and our master never uses a whip. I know a great deal and I can tell you there's no better place for a horse than this."

Ginger's Story

Squire Gordon took me for a ride the next day. My new master thought I rode very well and, when we returned to the stable, he praised me to John. Mrs. Gordon decided to name me Black Beauty—so I now had a new home and a fine new name!

A few days later I had to pull a carriage with Ginger. To my surprise, she behaved well. After a few trips, we grew quite friendly. I also became very good friends with Merrylegs. I was happy in my new home, but I missed my freedom. I always wore straps and blinkers and, for a young horse full of energy, not being able to run free was frustrating. Though on Sundays we spent time free in a field, as the carriage did not go out.

Over time, Ginger told me her story. She had never been shown kindness as a young horse, and her breaking-in was brutal and cruel. Her first home was with people who didn't care about horses, and Ginger had to wear a bearing rein that held her head painfully high. If she struggled, she was whipped. One day, she broke free of her harness, and after that she was sold.

The dealer treated her kindly, but then she went to another brutal master and soon became vicious again. Eventually, she was sold by the same dealer to Squire Gordon, who believed she could be saved. At last she was becoming confident and happy.

One day, Ginger, Merrylegs, and I were talking in
the orchard with another of Squire Gordon's horses,
Sir Oliver. He explained why he had such a short tail.

"When I was young, they cut off my beautiful tail, slicing
right through flesh and bone!" he snorted. It had hurt a lot
and it now meant that he could not brush away the flies
that landed on him. We were shocked at the cruelty of it,
especially as it was done purely for fashion.

I grew proud and happy living at Birtwick. Our master
was against all kinds of cruelty to horses and would not
put up with it. One day when he was riding me home,
we passed a workman driving a pretty pony. The pony
turned toward our path and the workman laid into him,
pulling the bit against his mouth and whipping him.
My master told him off, saying the pony only turned
that way from habit and that bad treatment would only
make his horse worse.

"You have often driven that pony up to my place and
the fact that he knows the way only shows good memory
and intelligence," he said sternly.

On another day, we met Captain Langley, a military friend
of my master's, driving his carriage with a pair of horses. Their
heads were held painfully high by a bearing rein. My master
encouraged him to think again about that fashion, saying:

"If your soldiers on parade had their heads held high
by force instead of holding them up high themselves,
you would not think they looked good."

A Stormy Day

One day, in late autumn, John hitched me to a light cart and we set off to drive my master to town. It was a terrible day, with howling wind and pouring rain. The river was swollen and the water had risen almost up to the wooden bridge.

On our way back, things were even worse. As we rode through the forest, there was a terrible crack and a crash, and a huge tree fell right across our path. I was terrified, but was too well behaved to panic and run. We had to go back to the crossroads and take another route, a good six miles longer.

When we finally got to the bridge, I would not set a hoof on it. My master touched me with the whip, but I knew better and stood still. John got down and came to talk to me, but still I would not stir. Although I could not say anything, I knew that I must not cross the bridge. Just then, the man who kept the bridge rushed out.

"Hey, stop!" he cried. "The bridge is broken in the middle and part of it is gone!"

John and my master were relieved and grateful. It took us a long time to get home, where the mistress was worried and looking out for us.

My master told her of our escape:
"We were almost swept away by the river, but clever Black Beauty saved us!"

The Fire

Another day, James drove Ginger and me on a long journey. We stopped for the night at an inn. The hostler—the man who looked after the horses there— took good care of us. During the night, we were woken by the arrival of a late traveler. The hostler prepared a stall for his horse and sent the traveler into the hayloft.

"Lay your pipe down there, and fetch some extra hay," the hostler said. The traveler fetched the hay, and we all went back to sleep. But I soon woke again. The air was thick and choking. Ginger was coughing and the other horses were restless and anxious. I soon realized the stable was full of smoke coming from the hayloft. I heard a strange crackling noise.

Footsteps approached, and the hostler threw the door open. In a panic, he began trying to drag the horses outside. Of course, his fear frightened us and we wouldn't move, so he left. The rush of fresh air from the door made it easier to breathe, but the crackling grew louder. I could see flickering red flames above us. After a few minutes, the hostler came back with James. They led the horses out gently.

"Come on, Beauty," James said, "it's time for us to go." He took me outside and ran back inside to rescue Ginger. We watched from a distance as the fire took hold and the stables burned down completely. Two poor horses that would not leave were burned to death.

Joe Green

James had found a new job as a groom at Clifford Hall and a young lad, Joe Green, was to replace him when he left. James thought him too inexperienced, but John said it was only fair to give him a chance. Soon, Joe started coming to the stables to learn from James. He was bright and cheerful, but Merrylegs grumbled at being "mauled about by a boy who knows nothing." At last, it was time for James to leave. He was very sad to go, and we were sad to lose him.

Only a few days later, I was woken in the night by the stable bell. The master insisted John go directly for the doctor, as the mistress was very ill. John chose me to ride on and we rode to the doctor's as fast as we could. I expected to rest, but the doctor rode me straight back to the manor as his own horse was exhausted. We made it back in good time. But only Joe was in the stable, and he didn't know how to deal with me. He didn't think to give me a warm blanket, and offered me a big pail of cold water, which I drank. Neither he nor I knew that was the wrong thing to do. After he'd gone, I began to shake and tremble with a terrible fever.

It was hours before John came and gave me warm food and blankets, and by then it was too late. By morning I was very ill and in great pain, and John had to nurse me day and night.

I do not know how long I was ill. The horse doctor came and my master visited me, too.

"My poor Beauty," he said, sad that my life had been risked. "Do you know you saved your mistress's life?"

I slowly recovered and Joe learned quickly after that. I grew to like him. One day, we saw a carter whipping his horses to pull a heavy load of bricks up a hill to a brick merchant's yard. Joe called to him to stop:

"Don't flog those horses like that! I'll help you to lighten the cart!"

But the carter told him to mind his own business and carried on. Joe rode me past him to the merchant's yard, where he reported what had happened. Later that day, the carter was brought before a magistrate. He heard Joe's evidence, and said the man must stand trial and perhaps go to prison.

When I had been at Birtwick for three years, the mistress became sick again. Eventually, the master decided they must all go to live in a warmer country. We were all sad. Merrylegs and Joe were to go to the minister. Ginger and I were to go and live with a friend of the master. John took us to our new home, a house called Earlshall. He told our new groom, Mr. York, that our master had never used the bearing rein with us.

"Well, if they come here," Mr. York said, "they must wear the bearing rein. My mistress likes her horses to hold their heads high."

The Bearing Rein

Luckily, York agreed to introduce the bearing rein slowly. It was my first experience of this sort of rein. I found it a nuisance, not being able to lower my head, but it held my head no higher than I would have held it myself.

The next day, though, our mistress told York, "Pull those horses' heads higher—they're not fit to be seen."

York told her it would be better to raise our heads slowly, and raised them just one notch on the rein. But, when we came to a steep hill, I could not put my head down to pull the carriage and it strained my back and legs.

"Now you see what I mean," Ginger said. "If it does not get much worse, we are lucky. But if it does, I won't bear it."

But each day, the rein was shortened a little more. I began to dread going into harness. At last, the rein stayed the same for several days and I thought the worst was over.

Then our mistress told York, "Pull those horses' heads up high, with no more nonsense!"

York pulled my head so high I could hardly bear it. Ginger reared up and thrashed so that she overturned the carriage and fell over. Ginger was never allowed to pull the carriage again, and I had a new partner, called Max. He told me how much damage the tight rein does to horse's windpipes, and I could certainly believe it.

Reuben Smith

There was a man who worked with York called Reuben Smith. He knew a great deal about horses and was good to us, but he had a bad habit of getting drunk.

One of the carriages was to be repaired, so Smith and I took it to the carriage-maker. Before we set off home, Smith took me to have a feed while he went for a drink. He came back very drunk. The hostler who had been caring for me told him I had a loose shoe, but Smith said it would be fine until we got back.

On our way home, though, my shoe worked itself loose and was causing me a lot of pain. My hoof was soon cut and my foot started bleeding. On a stretch of straight road, Smith used the whip to make me gallop. Eventually I stumbled—there was nothing I could do to prevent it—and Smith was thrown off and fell to the ground. He lay still in the road, and I waited a long time standing beside him.

Near midnight, a group of people sent from Earlshall found us. They were shocked that I had thrown Smith, until the groom, Robert, saw my foot. I later found out that Smith was dead and, at the inquest, the hostler told how he had warned him about the loose shoe. I was cleared of blame, but badly hurt. Both of my knees were damaged, and although the horse doctor did his best, they never fully recovered.

Life as a Job-horse

When my injuries healed, I was put into a meadow on my own. I was lonely for a long time, then Ginger joined me. She had been ruined by the master's son riding her too hard. She was to have a year in the meadow to see if she would recover. But the master said he could not have a horse with such damaged knees in the stable, and I was to be sold to a man in Bath.

I was to be a job-horse, rented out to anyone who needed a horse for their carriages. Often, I seemed to go to people who didn't know how to drive a horse. One day, I was sent out with a man who paid no attention to how I was going. I soon had a stone in my hoof, but he didn't notice anything until I was going lame with the pain. Luckily, a farmer rode by and told him there was something wrong. The farmer checked my hoof, found the stone and dug it out— with some trouble and pain because it had worked a far way in. He told the driver to use me gently, for my foot was very bruised. But, of course, the driver just grumbled and went back to our previous pace.

Some drivers treat horses like steam engines and expect them to start at full speed and go on without tiring. I met several horses who had been ruined by bad driving. But there were good drivers, too.

26

One man asked for the curb bit to be removed from my mouth, and that was much more comfortable. After he had driven me a few times, he asked if he might buy me for a friend, and that's how I came to live with Mr. Barry.

Mr. Barry did not know much about horses but he was kind and ordered everything I needed. But, his groom, Filcher, did not feed me properly. I grew weaker and weaker, and one day a farmer advised Mr. Barry to check on my diet.

"If you are paying for oats for this horse, he is not getting them," the farmer said.

I had often seen Filcher's son sneak in and fill a bag with oats from my bin. But the master called in the police and soon the boy was caught in the act. The boy was too young to be found guilty, but Filcher was sent to prison for two months.

The next groom was called Smirk. He was very polite and nice to me in front of the master, but he was lazy. He never cleaned my tackle or changed my straw or exercised me. Eventually, my feet were so infected and sore from standing on dirty, wet straw, that I stumbled when my master took me out.

The horse doctor told him what was wrong, and that I must be well exercised and kept clean. Mr. Barry was so disgusted at being cheated by two grooms in a row that he decided to give up keeping a horse, and so I was sold again.

A London Cab-horse

I was taken to a horse fair. There were horses of all shapes and sizes, and buyers of all sorts, too. A kind man came to look at me. He seemed pleasant and knowledgeable, and I would have been happy to go with him, but he didn't offer a high enough price. Then a hard and nasty-looking man started bargaining to buy me, and I was afraid. But we horses have no say in where we go. Luckily, the kind man returned and made a higher offer, so I went with him.

We went to London, where I met his young children who petted me. I thought I should be happy with them.

My new master was called Jerry. He and his family made a great fuss over me and I was very well cared for, but the work of a cab-horse is hard and it took me a while to get used to the bustle and noise of London. We had a rest day on Sundays, and we needed it.

One Sunday, I found out about my companion horse, Captain. He had been trained as a war horse, and had been to the Crimean War. He told me about the terrible conditions—about traveling over the sea on a ship, about the battlefields where men and horses alike were shot or injured, where the mud was slippery with blood and the cries of the wounded were terrifying.

During the war, Captain fought in many battles and saw much bloodshed. One day, his master was shot in battle. He fell to the ground, but Captain was swept along with the rush of the other horses, with no rider. Another soldier, whose horse had been shot, jumped on to his back.

"The groans of the wounded horses were dreadful to hear," he said. "And after the battle, a man with a pistol went around and shot all the horses that were injured."

Jerry had a good, regular customer called Mrs. Briggs. One day, a gentleman came to the cab rank and asked Jerry if he could fix a rate for taking Mrs. Briggs to church each Sunday. Jerry said he was sorry, but Sunday was our rest day and he spent it with his family. However much the man argued, Jerry refused. When he got home, Jerry told his wife, Polly, what he had decided. He was afraid that it would mean no more work from Mrs. Briggs, though. Polly said he was right to refuse. But the weeks passed and there were no more calls from Mrs. Briggs. Then finally one day Polly ran across the yard to tell Jerry that Mrs. Briggs had sent for him.

"She has tried other cabs, but there is always something wrong with them—and she would rather have you for six days of the week than none!" she said. So all was well again, and we worked for Mrs. Briggs, keeping our Sundays for ourselves.

Poor Ginger

One day, while my cab was waiting at a park, a shabby old cab pulled up, drawn by a skinny chestnut horse. To my horror, it was Ginger! She told me that she had spent a year in the meadow but had been sold several times since. Each new owner had over-worked her and she had become more and more broken. She had recently been bought as a cab-horse, but her owner soon realized her injuries meant she was not worth what he had paid for her.

"So he said I must just be used up," Ginger said, sadly. "And that is what they are doing. They are whipping and working me with no thought for what I suffer."

"But you used to stand up for yourself when you were maltreated," I said.

"I can't any more," Ginger replied. "If men are cruel, there is nothing we can do. We horses must just suffer and bear it. I wish I were dead. I have seen dead horses, and I don't think they suffer."

I was very much troubled, and I put my nose up to hers, but I could say nothing to comfort her. I think she was pleased to see me, though, for she said, "You are the only friend I have ever had."

A little while after this, I saw a cart carrying a dead horse. It was a chestnut with a white stripe on the forehead and I think it was Ginger. I hope it was.

34

Kind Deeds

It was election day. I had never seen an election before, and I don't think I want to see another. All the cabs were busy, and the streets crowded. Two people were knocked down in the street before my eyes.

As we paused at a cab stop, a woman came up carrying a small child and asked Jerry the way to the hospital.

"You can't get there on foot," Jerry said, "not through these crowds. Get in and I will take you."

"But I don't have enough money," the woman said. "Please, just tell me the way."

"You can't carry the child. I will take you for no charge. I have a wife and children of my own."

"Heaven bless you!" the woman said.

At the hospital, Jerry helped the woman out and then patted my neck, pleased to have helped.

The rain was now pouring down and, just as we were leaving, a lady came down the hospital steps wanting a cab. Jerry seemed to know her and it turned out that Polly had worked for her in the past.

"How do you find cab work in winter?" she asked him. Jerry told her that it was difficult in the bad weather and that he had been unwell. The lady said it was a shame to risk his health, and that if he ever wanted work as a driver or as a groom, he should contact her. She gave him five shillings for each of his two children and at last we could go home.

New Year's Eve

Christmas and New Year are busy times for cab-men. On New Year's Eve, we took some men to a card game. They asked us to return at eleven, but warned Jerry he might have to wait a few minutes. There was no sign of the men at eleven, and we waited in the cold, getting more and more chilled, until they finally came at a quarter past one. We then had to drive two miles in the bitter weather. I was so cold I almost stumbled, and the men did not thank us for waiting or apologize at all. Jerry's cough became worse and worse.

The next day, Jerry didn't come for me. His young son, Harry, came to feed me instead. I heard Harry talking to his sister, Dolly, and learned that Jerry was dangerously ill, the cold weather having affected him badly. A friend of Jerry's, Governor Grant, came to see how he was and offered to exercise the horses. At long last, Jerry began to get better, but the doctor said he could never return to cab work.

The woman we had picked up at the hospital, Mrs. Fowler, heard of Jerry's problem and offered him a job looking after her horses. And so it was settled. He was to sell the cab and horses and go to Mrs. Fowler. I never saw him again, but Polly and the children came and said good-bye, and cried and patted me fondly before they left.

Moving On

At first I was sold to a corn dealer. He was a good enough man himself, but had a harsh foreman who always made me pull loads that were too heavy. My driver, Jakes, objected, but the foreman said, "What is the point in going twice when you can go once? Just do it."

One day, I was struggling to pull an extremely heavy load up a steep hill and had to keep stopping. Jakes lashed me with a heavy whip every time, but there was nothing I could do—I was using every ounce of my strength. A passing lady interrupted us:

"Pray, don't whip your horse! I am sure he is doing his best."

But Jakes said, "If his best won't get us up the hill, it's not going to be good enough."

Then the lady explained that if Jakes removed the bearing rein and let me lower my head, I would be more able to pull the load. Jakes didn't believe the lady knew anything, but said he would try. Of course, it worked. I shook my head, glad to be free of the rein, and then pulled the load uphill. After that Jakes often took the rein off when we went uphill, and it helped a great deal.

But pulling very heavy loads day after day still wore me out and, after a few months, I was replaced with a younger horse and sold to a cab owner.

Hard Times

My new owner, Skinner, had black eyes, a hooked nose, and too many teeth. Everything I had heard about how cab-horses suffer, I now experienced. He worked me long and hard, with no day of rest, driving me with a cruel whip that drew blood. My life was so wretched that, like Ginger, I wished I could die.

One day, a family approached us at the railroad station. They had piles of luggage. The small girl pleaded with her father, "I'm sure this poor horse can't take all of our luggage." The porter suggested they take a second cab for the boxes, but Skinner said I could do it. Still the girl pleaded, but her father wouldn't listen.

"If the man says his horse can do it, he knows," he said crossly. But the girl was right. The load was heavy and my hooves skidded on the wet streets until, at last, I slipped and fell. As I lay on the ground, unable to move, I heard angry voices all around me. The little girl was crying, "Oh, the poor horse! It is all our fault!"

At first they thought I was dead but, eventually, I was roused and taken home. The horse doctor said I needed six months of rest, but Skinner wouldn't hear of it and said he'd sell me for meat instead. He was finally persuaded to give me a few days of rest before selling me. I held up my head and hoped for the best.

My Rescue

At the sale I was at the poor end with the old broken horses and among the men with little money. Some of these men were hardened by their cruel lives, but some still looked kind. A small boy, Willie, spotted me and begged his grandfather to consider me. He rightly judged that was I was not as old as I looked, and only needed good care.

"Couldn't you buy him and make him fit again?" the boy asked.

The farmer, Mr. Thoroughgood, looked at me carefully and finally agreed to buy me for five pounds. So I went to their farm, where Willie came to pet me each day in the meadow where I lived. Willie was in charge of me, and I had good feeds of hay and oats every night and morning. Slowly my strength returned with this kind treatment, and I felt I was indeed growing young and fit again. But when summer came, Thoroughgood said it was time to collect on his investment and sell me on.

"We must look for a quiet, gentle place, where he will be well looked after," he said to Willie.

For a few days I was trimmed and polished and made to look as glossy as possible. At last, Thoroughgood and Willie took me to meet two ladies who lived together in a pretty house. Thoroughgood recommended me to the ladies and offered them the chance to try me for a few days.

My Last Home

The ladies trusted Thoroughgood and agreed to a trial. Their groom noticed my poor knees though, and was concerned.

"I didn't think, sir, that you would recommend such a broken horse," he said.

"His knees have only been broken through ill-treatment," Thoroughgood said. "If the ladies are disappointed, they can return him to me."

So I was led to a comfortable stable. As the groom began to clean my face the next day, he said, "That is just like the star Black Beauty had on his face. I wonder where he is now?"

And then, as he found other marks on my body that he knew, he cried out, "Why, it must be Black Beauty! Beauty! Do you remember me? I am little Joe Green who almost killed you!"

I didn't recognize him, for he was now full-grown, but I did remember him. I put my nose up to him, and tried to say that we were friends. I was so happy to see him again. He told the ladies my story and they agreed to keep me. They wrote to Squire Gordon's wife to tell her that they had her favorite horse, and they promised never to sell me. Thoroughgood and Willie visited and said that with good treatment I might live for quite a few years more. So, at last, I have found a happy home where my troubles are over, and my story ends here.

About the Author

Anna Sewell was born in 1820 in Norfolk, England. At the age of 14 she fell while running in the rain, and badly injured both of her ankles. Anna never walked properly again. Because of this, she often rode horses and drove her own carriage and her love of horses grew. In 1871, Anna started writing *Black Beauty*—a story to encourage better treatment of horses—but it took her seven years to complete the book, as she became more and more unwell. *Black Beauty* was Anna's only book and, sadly, she never got to enjoy its success. Anna died in 1878, just five months after *Black Beauty* was published.

Other titles in the *Classic Collection* series:

The Adventures of Tom Sawyer • *Alice's Adventures in Wonderland* • *Black Beauty*
Gulliver's Travels • *Heidi* • *Little Women* • *Pinocchio* • *Robin Hood*
Robinson Crusoe • *The Secret Garden* • *The Three Musketeers*
Treasure Island • *The Wizard of Oz* • *20,000 Leagues Under The Sea*

402 Industrial Lane
Birmingham, Alabama 35211

© 2014 by QEB Publishing

This 2014 edition published by Sweet Water Press by arrangement with QEB Publishing.

QED PROJECT EDITOR: Alexandra Koken
MANAGING EDITOR: Victoria Garrard • **DESIGN MANAGER:** Anna Lubecka
EDITOR: Louise John • **DESIGNER**: Rachel Clark

ISBN-13: 978 1 49241 653 1

Printed in China

2 4 6 8 10 9 7 5 3 1